This book belongs to:

ALEG BRADY

looking forward
to seeing you at
in Africa!
where the wild
animals are........

MR BENN'S BIG GAME

For Emma, Will and Tom

MR BENN'S BIG GAME

DAVID MCKEE

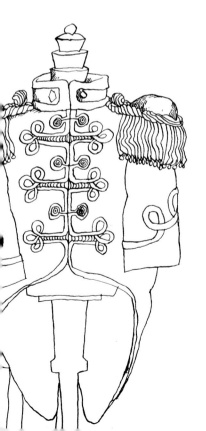

This edition first published in 2021 by Andersen Press Ltd.,
20 Vauxhall Bridge Road, London SW1V 2SA
First published as *Big Game Benn* by Dobson, London in 1979
Copyright © David McKee, 1979
The right of David McKee to be identified as the author and illustrator of this work
has been asserted by him in accordance with the Copyright, Designs and Patents Act, 1988.
All rights reserved. Printed and bound in China.
10 9 8 7 6 5 4 3 2 1
British Library Cataloguing in Publication Data available.
ISBN 978 1 83913 071 7

Mr Benn sat in the park at the end of Festive Road. He fed the birds and thought. He thought about a special costume shop that he knew, a shop that adventures could start from. He thought about the adventures he had had and he remembered a hat that he had thought of trying on at the end of his last adventure. That made him think that it was time he visited the shop again.

It was not long before he was in the shop and looking at the hat he had remembered. As he picked it up, as if by magic, the shopkeeper appeared.

"Good morning, sir," he said, "it is nice to see you again. Can I help you?"

"Good morning," said Mr Benn holding up the hat. "Is there an outfit to go with this hat?"

The shopkeeper smiled and took down a box from the shelf. Inside the box were some khaki clothes.

"Why don't you see if they fit, sir?" said the shopkeeper.

Mr Benn took the outfit into the little fitting room with all its mirrors. He changed and saw that it was a kind of a hunter's outfit. He tried different poses and admired himself then went to the door, not the one that led back to the shop but the one marked TRYING ROOM. He went through the door wondering where it would lead him this time.

Mr Benn walked through the door and came out from a tent into an open space in a jungle. Nearby stood a group of men all dressed like Mr Benn but – all of them had guns. The man who seemed to be the leader called out as soon as he saw Mr Benn, "Ah, there you are! You must be our guide. Well, come on. Lead the way. Find us some animals to shoot."

"Animals to shoot?" thought Mr Benn. "What an awful idea." But he said nothing and started to walk through the jungle. The hunters followed.

As they walked the leader of the hunters boasted to Mr Benn. "You know," he said, "you're very lucky to be guiding us, we must be the greatest hunters who ever lived. Here I'll show you," and with that he aimed his gun at a bird. That worried Mr Benn and quickly he said, "Surely if you are such a great hunter you don't bother with little birds?"

"What?" said the hunter. "Oh, no, of course not!" And he pretended that he hadn't intended to shoot. The bird was left in peace.

A little later a snake crossed their path. Mr Benn saw the hunter start to raise his gun and said, "I don't suppose an expert like you bothers with snakes either?"

"Ah, eh! Oh, no! Oh no, no, no!" blustered the hunter. "I was just... I was just... I was trying my sights!" And he raised and lowered the gun a few times as if he were practising.

After that they came to a small hill that rose out of the jungle. On top of the hill stood a deer.

"Now there is something to shoot," said one of the men.

"What?" said Mr Benn scornfully. "That's not nearly big enough! We'll find something worthwhile in a minute." And he led the men on into the jungle.

They kept walking until they came to a river. They sat there and rested, watching the fish. Fortunately the hunters didn't even consider shooting the fish. Mr Benn noticed a crocodile asleep across the river. "Look!" he said and pointed. "There's a crocodile, but of course we can find something much larger than that!" When the hunters went on their way again the crocodile slept on undisturbed.

Next they surprised a lion as it lay outside its cave. "Not large enough! Not large enough! Not large enough!" sang out Mr Benn and dismissed the lion with a wave of his hand as he led the men on their way.

Not long after that they passed through a valley where a giraffe was standing. Mr Benn looked it up and down thoughtfully.

"Hmmm, yes. It's certainly tall," he admitted. And then added hastily, "But no, no, it's not fat enough! No, not big enough for the greatest big game hunters!"

Still no shots had been fired as once again Mr Benn headed the little party through the jungle.

By now the hunters were hungry so they stopped at the next clearing to eat their sandwiches. While they were busy eating, a hippo wandered by. As soon as the men saw the big animal they started for their guns.

"STOP!" shouted Mr Benn. "I know that hippo is big but it's not the biggest animal, and only the biggest is good enough for the greatest big game hunters."

"That's right," they said. "The biggest for the greatest!" With self-satisfied smiles they settled to finish their sandwiches.

After lunch the hunters decided to have a little rest before going on with the hunt. That suited Mr Benn very well because he wanted to think.

While the men slept he went for a thinking walk. So far he had managed to stop any of the animals from getting hurt but how would it all end?

As Mr Benn walked he felt that the ground was shaking under his feet. The farther he walked the greater the shaking grew. In the end the shaking became so bad that Mr Benn fell over. As he fell over he saw a herd of elephants, a herd of shaking elephants. They weren't shaking because the ground was, it was their shaking that was making the ground bounce up and down. Suddenly Mr Benn realised that the elephants were all shaking with fear.

Carefully Mr Benn crawled along the bouncing ground to the elephants.

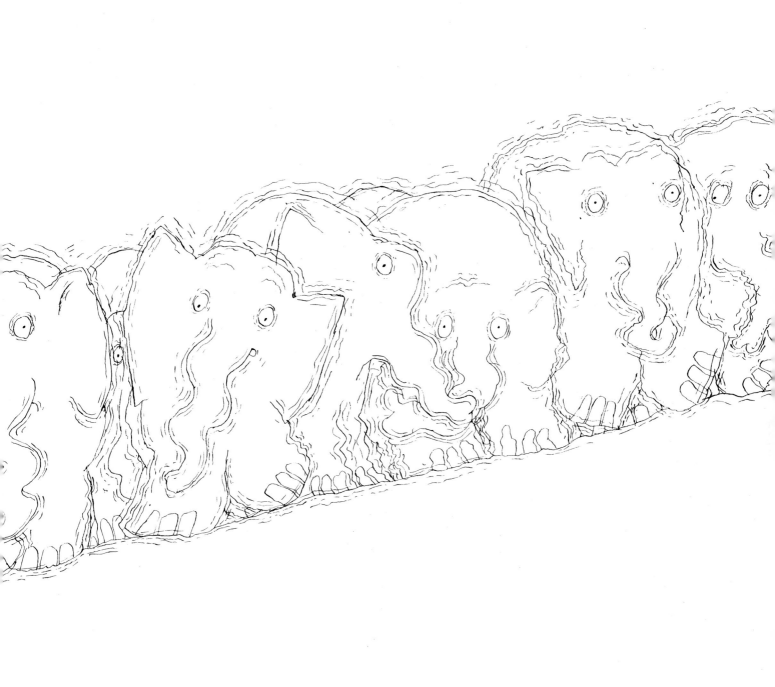

Once there he managed to calm them down enough for him to be able to stand up and talk to them. "It's very good the way you have managed to save the other animals," said one of the elephants. "But, oh dear, oh dear, what will happen to us? We are the biggest, the biggest for the greatest big game hunters. We are bound to be shot."

"I've been worrying about the same thing," said Mr Benn, "but you have just given me an idea. Listen!" The elephants crowded round and listened to Mr Benn's plan. When he left they felt much happier.

Mr Benn returned to the hunters and woke them with a shout. "Come on! Come on quickly! I've found just the thing!" He almost dragged the still sleepy leader through the jungle and the others followed as fast as they could. Mr Benn led the way straight to the clearing where the elephants stood. "Look!" he said. "Just the thing! The biggest animals for the greatest big game hunters!"

Rubbing the last of the sleep from their eyes the delighted hunters raised their guns. At the same time Mr Benn sat down. That was the signal for the elephants. They started to jump up and down for all they were worth. How the ground shook. The hunters didn't have a chance. Every shot they fired went either into the air or into the ground, and that went on until every last shot had been fired.

The elephants were untouched and when the shooting finished they walked happily away. Mr Benn scolded the hunters as if they had been naughty. "Call yourselves great hunters? You can't even hit an elephant! You're not safe with guns!" Then a little more kindly he said, "Why don't you get rid of the guns? Hunt and shoot with cameras instead, then if you miss at least you'll get a picture of something."

After that the hunters were quiet and thoughtful as Mr Benn led the way back to the camp and there, believe it or not, was a camera salesman. Mr Benn thought that he recognised the man but before he could say anything he was asked to put the things in the tent and then help to choose cameras. He went into the tent and found that he was back in the changing room of the shop. There, on the floor, were his own clothes.

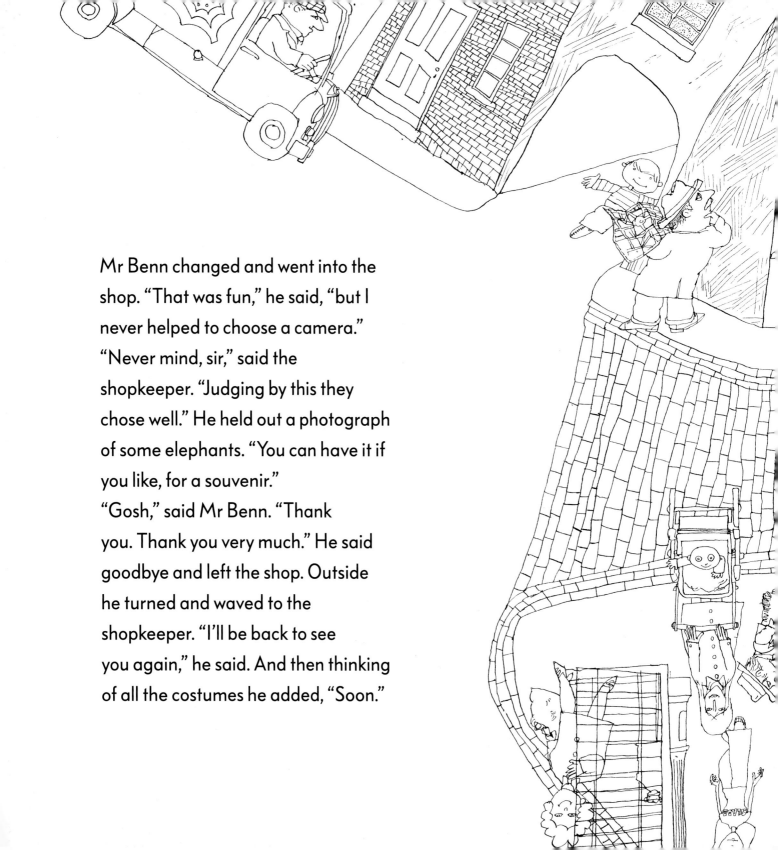

Mr Benn changed and went into the shop. "That was fun," he said, "but I never helped to choose a camera." "Never mind, sir," said the shopkeeper. "Judging by this they chose well." He held out a photograph of some elephants. "You can have it if you like, for a souvenir."

"Gosh," said Mr Benn. "Thank you. Thank you very much." He said goodbye and left the shop. Outside he turned and waved to the shopkeeper. "I'll be back to see you again," he said. And then thinking of all the costumes he added, "Soon."

Collect the original Mr Benn books!